"Maybe Goldie could visit the aquarium?" says Mummy Pig. An aquarium is a place where there are lots of fish.

Peppa and her family
drive to the aquarium.

"I hope we can find a friend
for Goldie," says Peppa.
"I'm sure we will," snorts Daddy Pig.
"The aquarium has every type of fish!"

Peppa Pig

Peppa's Fishy Friends

Goldie is Peppa's pet fish. Today she looks a bit sad.
"I think Goldie is lonely," says Peppa.
"She hasn't got any fishy friends."

Miss Rabbit works at the aquarium.
"Welcome, everyone!" she says.

"Does the aquarium have every type of fish?" asks Peppa. "Oh yes," replies Miss Rabbit. "Probably."

The tanks in the first room are full of tiny fish.

Peppa starts to sing.
"Fishy, fishy, fish,
fish, swimming
in the sea!
Who will be a
fishy friend for
my Goldie?"

"Could any of these fish be Goldie's friend?" asks Daddy Pig.

Peppa and Goldie look through the glass.
"No," decides Peppa. "They are too small."

Peppa tries the next room.
Candy Cat is there with her
mummy and daddy.

Candy's family come
to the aquarium all the time.
"It's better than watching
TV!" Mrs Cat beams.
"We like fish!" adds Mr Cat.

"What's in this tank?"
asks Mummy Pig.
Daddy Pig jumps back.
The fish in this tank
is very big.

"This fish is too big to
be friends with Goldie,"
decides Peppa.

"Whoa!"

There's something
funny in the next tank.
"Dine-saw!"
growls George.
"It's not a dinosaur,"
says Mummy Pig.
"It's a funny kind of
fish called a seahorse."

Peppa thinks that
the seahorse is too
much like a dinosaur
to be Goldie's friend.

There's only one room left. This tank
is covered in green slime.

"Hello!"

"There's a fish with big long ears!" gasps Daddy Pig. "It's a rabbit fish!"

Peppa laughs. It is only Miss Rabbit wearing a diving costume! She is cleaning the glass.

There are no more fish tanks. Peppa takes Goldie into the aquarium café.

"Hello," says Miss Rabbit. "Did you find a friend for Goldie?"
"No," sighs Peppa.

Peppa spots a fish on
Miss Rabbit's counter.
"That's just Ginger," says
Miss Rabbit. "My pet goldfish."

"My fish isn't lonely any more!" Peppa laughs. Goldie has found her friend.

Collect these other great Peppa Pig stories